W9-ASJ-124

SESAME STREET ®
A GROWING-UP BOOK ™

It's No Fun to Be Sick!

By CAROLINE BARNES
Illustrated by TOM BRANNON

A SESAME STREET/GOLDEN PRESS BOOK

Published by Western Publishing Company, Inc., in conjunction with Children's Television Workshop.

©1989 Children's Television Workshop. Sesame Street puppet characters ©1989 Jim Henson Productions, Inc. All rights reserved. Printed in the U.S.A. No part of this book may be reproduced or copied in any form without written permission from the publisher. Sesame Street®, the Sesame Street sign®, and a GROWING-UP BOOK are trademarks and service marks of Children's Television Workshop. All other trademarks are the property of Western Publishing Company, Inc. Library of Congress Catalog Card Number: 88-81485 ISBN: 0-307-12031-9/ISBN: 0-307-62031-X (lib. bdg.)

MCMXCII

It was a beautiful afternoon on Sesame Street. Herry Monster raced home from school. There was still plenty of time to play outside before dinner.

"I'm home, everybody!" Herry shouted. He grabbed his favorite red ball and went into the kitchen.

"Hello, Herry dear," said Mommy Monster, giving him a kiss. "Your sister is asleep. She has a fever and a sore throat. Dr. Fuzzy says she should stay in bed."

"Oh, no," said Herry. "I wanted her to play catch with me. Oh, well. I'll go outside anyway."

Herry went out into the backyard. He tossed the ball
high into the air. He tried to catch it, but it landed right
in the middle of a prickly rosebush.

"Ouch!" said Herry when he reached a furry arm in
to get his ball.

In the sandbox, Herry wiggled his big furry toes in the sand. Flossie liked to bury his feet in the sand. She always laughed when he pulled them out. Today the sandbox was no fun without Flossie.

Herry went back inside. It was time for his favorite TV show, *My Little Monster*. But the television set was gone!

"Mommy," called Herry, "where is the TV?"

"In Flossie's room," Mommy answered. "She wanted to watch *Captain Koala* before her nap."

"May I watch TV, too?" Herry asked.

"Yes," said Mommy. "But not until Flossie wakes up."

Herry went to his room and took out his blocks.
Mommy stuck her head in the door. "Shhh," she said.
"Remember, Flossie is asleep!"

Herry decided to build a block tower. He stacked the
blocks and the tower grew taller and taller. Then he
gave the rug a tug—and the tower fell down with a crash!

In the next room, Flossie began to cry.

Herry ran into Flossie's room. "Hi, Flossie," he said.
"Want to play ball?"

Flossie sat up. She was wearing Mommy's silk bed
jacket. "No!" she said.

Mommy hurried in. "How are you feeling, darling?
Would you like some warm cranberry juice?"

Flossie frowned. "Yes," she said, "with orange slices in it."

"Oh, dear," said Mommy. "It's no fun to be sick! It makes
Flossie as grouchy as Oscar."

Mommy brought Flossie a cup of warm cranberry juice on a tray.

"May I have some, too?" asked Herry.

Mommy shook her head. "It would spoil your dinner, Herry."

"But Flossie gets to have some now," said Herry.

"Flossie is sick," Mommy reminded him. "This will make her feel better."

Later Mrs. Scary came by with a book for Flossie. On the cover was a big furry monster. "Oh, let me see that!" said Herry when she left.

"It's for Flossie, Herry," Mommy said. "I'm sure she will share it with you later."

When Daddy came home, Herry ran to greet him with a big hug.

"Will you play Monsterland with me?" asked Herry.

"Not right now, Herry," said Daddy. "I want to see how Flossie's feeling."

"How's my sick little monster?" asked Daddy after Mommy gave Flossie some pink medicine in a cup.

"Terrible," said Flossie.

"Would it help if I read you a story?" asked Daddy.

"Yes," said Flossie. "Read me my new book."

"Come and listen, Herry," said Daddy.

Herry shook his head. "I think I'll just play in my room," he said.

That night, after Mommy tucked Herry in bed, he hugged his dolly. "I wish I could be sick," he whispered. "Then I could watch TV in bed, and eat on a tray, and everyone would be extra nice to me."

He took a sip of water from a glass on his bed table and pretended it was pink medicine like Flossie's. Then he fell asleep.

The next morning Herry woke up early. He felt so warm that he kicked off his blankets. But a few minutes later he felt so cold that he began to shiver. "Mommy!" he called.

Mommy Monster hurried into his room. "What's the matter, Herry?" she asked.

"I feel awful," moaned Herry.

Mommy put her hand on Herry's furry forehead. "I hope you're not sick, too!" she said. Then she went to get a thermometer.

"Now open your mouth," said Mommy, "and put this
thermometer under your tongue. It will tell me if you
have a fever."

In three minutes Mommy took it out and looked at it
closely. "Oh, dear," she said. "I think you have the same
thing that Flossie has. You will have to stay in bed
today."

Before he left for work, Daddy put the television set in Herry's room. But Herry couldn't watch it. His head hurt too much.

Mommy brought Herry a banana yogurt shake. But Herry couldn't drink it. His throat hurt too much.

Mommy covered Herry with a special soft quilt made by Grandma Monster. But the quilt only made Herry feel warmer, so he pushed it away.

That night Mommy gave Herry a cupful of the pink medicine. "Dr. Fuzzy says this will help you get better, Herry," she said.

"Yucch!" he said. "That tastes terrible."

Mommy kissed him good night. "You'll feel better soon," she said softly.

Herry wished it were soon.

The next morning Herry woke up with Flossie
jumping up and down on his bed.

"Let's play in the sandbox, Herry. Come on!" she
shouted.

Herry's throat was still sore. His head still ached.
"Stop it, Flossie!" he grumbled. "And don't make so
much noise."

Mommy brought Herry his medicine. "Flossie," she said, "you must leave Herry alone. He needs to rest."

"But, Mommy," said Flossie, "I want Herry to play with me."

Mommy shook her head. "Not today, Flossie."

Herry watched sadly as Flossie ran out to play with the kids next door. He wanted to play, too. But he ached all over.

That afternoon Herry ate his favorite lunch, chicken soup and crackers, on a tray, but it didn't taste good. Later, when Daddy Monster read him a story, he felt too tired to listen.

"I think I'll go to sleep now," he told Mommy after dinner.

Herry felt tired and achy for three days. Then one morning his throat wasn't sore anymore.

Mommy was in the kitchen making Flossie's breakfast. "Do you feel better, Herry?" she asked.

"Ya," he said. "I feel like having some Monsterberry Crunch! Then let's go out and play, Flossie!"

In the sandbox, Flossie dumped a bucket of sand on Herry's feet. Herry wiggled his furry toes until they poked through the sand. Flossie laughed.

"This is fun!" said Herry. "It's no fun to be sick!"